The Scroll of Isidor

HOLDEN SHEPPARD

ISBN: 9781370570416

DEDICATION

This story is dedicated to my D&D crew: Rael, Lidda and our excellent, slightly biased DM. You all know who you are.

I also dedicate this to our hapless, mostly useless NPC, Sildar.

ACKNOWLEDGMENTS

I would like to acknowledge the help of my beta readers, Joshua Boyle and Adam Friday, who gave me valuable advice in shaping this story.

I also must thank my fantastic, hawk-eyed editor, Georgina Gregory of Plume. She can spot a consistency error from ten paces, and helped make this story as strong as it is.

Finally, many thanks to my designer, Angie, who did a phenomenal job with the front cover design. I have lost count of how many people have sent me messages complimenting this brilliant book cover.

The Scroll of Isidor

HOLDEN SHEPPARD

Dervine, Eastern Flaran

For the past seven years, Lev had come to associate knocking on the Chief's knotted wooden door with a sense of suffocated dread.

This night was no different.

Lev shivered. The corridor that led to the Chief's Den was just as cold as the outside. Magnus always insisted on leaving the window open for carrier Pekrons, though it had been years since anything exciting enough had happened for someone to employ one of the messenger birds in the middle of the night.

Lev glanced through the window, half-hoping to see a flutter of deep purple feathers and the guttural, hypnotic croon, but no Pekron arrived. All that was visible beyond the window was the moon: a distant, tired slice of lunate light dangling in the navy sky above, waiting for dawn.

An icy gust blew unfettered through the window. Lev drew his black Furnik-hair cloak more tightly around his shoulders, re-fastening the single button that always insisted on unclipping itself, and rapped three times on the door to the Chief's Den.

The growl came through the door like the Chief was half-asleep. 'Not now, *jecarro.*'

The dialect word for 'young one' soured Lev's tongue. At twenty-nine, he may have been young for a deputy, but there was nothing juvenile about his war record. He sneered instinctively, glad of the protection the door offered.

'Chief Magnus, it's important.'

'Really, *jecarro*? Run out of bloodvine? Cellar key's under the mat.'

Rage flooded Lev's veins. He pounded the flat of his fist against the door. 'Chief, I've had a report of a rumbling in the mountain caves. Might be a wild Arkod. Worse, maybe another beast. We need to investigate. Slay it, if necessary.'

Something wooden clattered to the floorboards inside the Chief's den. A grunt of effort. Heavy, laboured footsteps. The metal bolt was thrown with a clank; the door swung open.

Chief Magnus stood in the doorway, a thick silken gown draped around his wide shoulders, exposing a hairy chest and enormous, flabby gut. Crumbs of something Lev didn't remember bringing him clung to the hairy trail between his protruding belly button and the strained line of his slip. The soft, pale feet of a young woman stuck out from the mountain of woollen bedclothes on his bed.

The Chief's face was thunderous. His bulbous nose was ruddier than usual – almost a luminescent scarlet.

'I am your Chief, *jecarro*,' he growled. 'Don't you think I read the scrolls that come across my desk? I do. And I talk to the other Chiefs, and the Halo, too. I know more than you know about this – and everything else!'

Lev's face burned, but he kept his face steady, teeth gritted. 'If something is rumbling in the mountains, we should know what it is. The village might be in danger. It is our job to protect Dervine, sir.'

Magnus feigned a look of surprise, then pressed a meaty hand to his belly. He burped unceremoniously; a stream of rancid air flew across Lev's face.

'It is *my* job, *jecarro*. You are my deputy. You're here to do what I tell you to do. And I'm telling you now not to worry about the noises in the mountains.'

'Then what are they?' Lev shot back. 'Tell me what's going on out there.'

Magnus wiped his nose. 'Do you remember how the Battle of the Bordunn Bridge ended, *jecarro*?'

Lev clenched his fist. 'You know I do, Chief.'

'That night, I was in the Neutral Tent with King Rowan and King Silas and the other advisers.' Magnus sniffed. 'We stayed up until dawn, brokering the peace deal, so that no more blood would be spilt between Flaran and Peterin. And we did it. I did it.' He narrowed his eyes, but his chapped lips curled. 'Where were you that night, again, *jecarro*?'

'In the infirmary, though I don't remember it,' Lev said quickly. He only had tales from his comrades to confirm what had caused the scars he'd lived with ever since. 'I nearly broke my body rescuing the villagers when the bridge collapsed.'

'Precisely!' Magnus boomed, wildly indifferent to the mention of Lev's renowned feat of heroism. 'Because you are a soldier. You went into battle when we told you and you retreated when we told you because you follow orders. The orders *I* give.' His eyes narrowed into piercing slits. 'I'm the Chief. When you need to know what's happening in the mountains, I'll tell you. Until then, go back to your lookout post. Drink some bloodvine if it keeps you calm. Stop being such a panicked little princess about everything.'

'Chief, if this is serious, we may need to –'

'Enough!' Magnus snapped. He scratched his belly, then brought his meaty hands together, rubbing his palms in a slow, methodical manner until a soft green light began to glow between them. 'For now, this is all you need my magic for.'

The green light sparked between his hands, elongating into lithe lariats of light. Magnus smirked and twirled his finger in a circular motion; the lariats began swirling, layering over one another, until the glow began to subside.

He had conjured a petite crown of flowers, the kind a girl would wear at her Ascendance ceremony: frail green stems, peppered with the signature periwinkle flowers of Dervine.

Magnus grasped the crown and jammed it onto Lev's head, tousling his long brown hair.

'There we go. A pretty crown for a pretty princess.'

He chuckled to himself and without another word, swung the door closed.

Fury pounded through Lev's bloodstream – a fury he was tired of swallowing. He strode to the end of the corridor and grabbed the window frame, jamming it shut. Let the old bastard complain about it tomorrow. He'd had enough. Annoying the Chief was the only thing that gave him pleasure these days.

And no Pekrons were coming, anyway.

Lev charged down the staircase, sword bouncing along by his side, his boots clomping on the wood. The casual mention of the Battle of the Bordunn Bridge made his blood boil. His actions that night had saved dozens of villagers' lives and earned him the post of Deputy Chief, yet it was Magnus who crowed about his role in ending the war.

Lev wished he'd been in the Neutral Tent that night. He was sure Magnus had sat on his backside and remained taciturn, stuffing his face with mead and salted leknuts, while the other leaders negotiated the terms of peace.

When Lev reached the entry chamber of the Chief's cabin, he saw Desma was still crouched by the fireplace, arms folded.

'I told you to leave,' he called flatly. Did nobody in this town respect him anymore?

The young woman's gaze flicked to just above his eyes. 'That's a pretty crown, Lev. Have you got a date for your Ascendance ceremony yet?'

Lev's face was scorching. He yanked the stupid crown off his head and, in a swift movement he hoped would impress, pulled his sword from its hilt, tossed the crown into the air and looped it around the sword's tip.

He marched deftly to Desma's side, proffering the crown at blade's length.

'A gift from me to you,' he said suavely.

A reluctant smile curled Desma's soft lips. 'You know me better than that, Lev. I'm not one for adornments.'

She wasn't wrong: her brown cloak covered an equally drab grey tunic. Desma never dressed up – she said the decorations so loved by most women only got in the way of her work on the orchard. But she was a radiant woman all the same: there was a fierce pledge behind her green eyes, a tough beauty in her cheeks.

'It's rude to refuse a gift,' Lev said, stomach squirming not uncomfortably.

He lifted the crown of twigs and flowers from the sword – already the green stems were crusting into brown wood – and placed it gently atop Desma's mane of auburn hair.

'Now, you should leave, like I said.'
'What did Magnus say?'

'You mean Chief Magnus.'
'Don't play with me, Lev.'
Lev steeled himself. 'We already knew about the mountains. I had to check with the Chief if we were allowed to tell you. Unfortunately, that information is privileged.'

'Privileged!' Desma scowled. 'Are you talking about the information or that useless, fat slob upstairs?'

Lev fought a smile away. He couldn't be seen to indulge such insults, but he also no longer had it in him to demand the villagers respect their Chief: he had lost that respect long ago.

'Leave it with us. Just go back to your orchard. Your brothers will be awake in a few hours.'

Desma's eyes flashed.

'Yes, my little brothers!' she cried. 'Josip is only nine. What am I supposed to tell him if those men finally break through the mountain? What if they're criminals – thieves or murderers? Do I tell him that our Chief is a fat waste of space, too lazy to defend us? Or should I say that our Deputy, the once great Levin Ruck, is now too much of a coward to stand up to him?'

Lev winced. She always seemed to see right through his bluster. He'd known it was hardly believable to pretend he'd known all along.

But saving face was no longer the most important thing.

'How do you know there are men up there?' he asked quickly. 'You said there were *noises* in the mountains. I assumed it was a wild Arkod.'

'I said "noises" and you ran up that staircase before I could say anything else!' Desma said. 'I assure you, it's not wild. Not an Arkod, nor any other beast. It's men.'

Lev's heart pounded. 'Men from *where?*'

'Exactly. That's why I came here as quickly as I could. They're tunnelling through the mountain. I can hear them.'

Lev glanced at the spiral staircase back to Magnus' den. A second attempt to sway him to action would not fare well. Sod him. Sod everything about him. Lev had dedicated his name – the name of his ancestors – to protecting Dervine. To disgrace his oath because of Magnus' short-sightedness was not an option.

The former soldier straightened his back and sheathed his sword. 'I'll be whipped if you're wrong, you know,' he said.

'What about backup?' Desma asked. 'If there are men in the mountain, don't you think you should meet force with force?'

'No backup,' Lev said. 'If I'm to abandon my post in direct defiance of the Chief's orders, it's best we keep it to ourselves. As reliable as my men are, they are also gossips, every last one of them. It would get back to Magnus. No. We'll ride to the mountain, just the two of us. Scope it out. And once we have proof, I can get the Chief to act.'

'Not even Eddren?'

'Eddy? Never!' Lev laughed. 'I love the man like a brother, but he's got the biggest mouth of them all. I swear to you, soldiers are as gossipy as old washer women.'

Desma raised an eyebrow and, subconsciously it seemed, touched her hand to the floral crown on her head. 'It's funny you say that,' she said. 'I just had the thought the other day that those washer women are even more vicious than soldiers.'

Lev opened the heavy oak cabinet at the rear of the room, where his light armour was stored among the thick loops of rope and other tools. Apart from training days and the occasional scuffle with Arkods or drunken travellers, he had scarcely needed it since the war.

He picked up the cuirass encrusted with sharp steel studs and looped it over his head, shifting the brown leather armour until it fitted snugly over his tunic. Putting on armour was always a powerful, exciting sensation; Lev always felt like his muscles had doubled in size.

But the armour was also tainted, bringing back the sounds and smells of the war with every metallic jingle of the buckles and every whiff of stale sweat seeping out of the tough leather.

A hand moved across Lev's back, snapping a buckle into place.

'I could've done that myself,' he said.

'You looked miles away,' Desma scoffed, clipping a second buckle. 'I was hoping we could get to the mountain before we're all slaughtered, if it's all the same to you?'

Lev hid his smirk and adjusted his steel-studded pauldrons.

'If I'm not going in with backup, I at least need to be armoured,' he said. 'Actually …' A smile softened his scarred features. 'What am I saying? I have the best backup there is. I have the girl who shoved Lord Aksel face-first into the Jadepool because he wouldn't let her go for a ride on his horse.'

Desma snorted ingloriously. 'I can't believe you remember that!'

'Are you kidding? That was one of the funniest moments of my childhood. Lord Aksel was such a pompous ass. Did your parents ever punish you for it?'

'They made a big fuss in front of everyone,' Desma said, doing up another buckle. 'But when we got back to the orchard, my father sat me down to scold me and then couldn't stop laughing. I think he liked seeing Aksel floundering around like a drunken eel as much as everyone else.'

Lev wrapped his favourite gauntlet around his wrist – it was made of an emerald-green leather – and began to lace it up. 'I remember thinking that day that I never wanted to get on your bad side.'

'Oh, you couldn't have. Not back then. The whole reason I wanted to ride Lord Aksel's horse was to join you and the others for your ride. You were handsome then, Lev. Blue eyes and broad shoulders.'

'Before my ugly mug got all cut up, you mean?' Lev traced the long scar on his face.

'I never said you weren't handsome now,' Desma said.

Lev's stomach curled itself into a lump. 'God's arse, Desma. I can see why the washer women talk about you.'

'Oh, don't worry, Lev. They talk about you too.'

'Really? What do they say?'

'Can't tell, I'm afraid. Woman's honour.' A devilish glint twinkled in Desma's green eyes. 'It's all bad, though.'

Lev finished pulling his boots on and fought a smile away. It had been a long time since he and Desma had spoken like this, and he missed it.

'Stands to reason,' he said gruffly. 'Deputies never get the respect we deserve.'

He stood up.

'It's time. Let's get to the horses.'

#

The two horses galloped up the winding track that meandered along the side of the Dervine Range. Desma led the way, the hood of her drab cloak blown down by the icy wind, flaming hair streaming out behind her; whether she'd stowed the floral crown or it had blown off, Lev didn't know. Desma's mare was a sinewy Kostish, probably from Kaltfross. Its coat was nearly as white as the patches of snow that streaked the ledges of the mountains to their right.

'Come on, Huck, keep up!' Lev called, digging his knees into his stallion's black-and-brown flank.

The horse grunted with effort and redoubled his speed, but only for a few paces, eventually falling into a comfortable canter behind the Kostish. Huck still had some life in him, but his war days really were a distant memory now.

As they rounded the boulder known as Rock of Rekkor, Lev narrowed his eyes against the biting wind and turned his gaze to the left. The village of Dervine was spread out in the valley below, most of the huts and houses in shadow, the spire in the centre of town a silhouette against the sky. The moonlight threw Desma's orchard into sharp relief.

What do these men want with Dervine? Lev wondered, setting his jaw in anxiety. Were they foreign merchants who got badly lost en route to Bordunn? Criminals who roamed the mountain passes to scam passers-by? Local men doing something untoward that Lev had been excluded from?

The only other option was the one that didn't add up. Beyond the mountains was the border with Peterin. The nearest civilisation on the opposite side of the mountain was Paik Ford, an allied alpine village several miles away that, despite being within Peterin's borders, had never taken up arms against Dervine, even during the war. That said, the mountainous terrain made contact between the villages infrequent. Could they be trying to make contact now?

'In here!' Desma shouted from ahead.

Lev returned his attention to the path. Rounding the Rock of Rekkor had led them to a rocky clearing that pressed into the side of the mountain. Evergreen ivy leaves crept over every surface, choking the rocky outcrops and snaking through the patches of slushy snow.

Desma had paused at the far side of the clearing, where a dark opening led to the caves.

'We need a light,' she called. Her face was rosy, partly from the cold and partly from a dignified obstinacy. Lev knew she didn't like drawing attention to her weakness as a mage.

'I'll do the honours,' he called back. 'Huck, wait – no, wait, I say.'

Once Huck was settled, Lev drew his sword, the steel glinting in the pallid moonlight. He twisted his index finger in a few quick circles around the sword's tip. Soft emerald light erupted in a thin jet from his finger, twirling around the sword's tip until it formed a small orb of light, clinging to the tip of the blade.

'You make it look so easy,' Desma said stiffly, hugging her cloak closer. 'Mine always comes out a horrible yellow. Barely lights up anything.'

'Not every mage steals the stage,' Lev said fairly. It was an old maxim, meant to reassure late bloomers and weaker mages that their powers, while not as ostentatious as those of warrior mages, were still of value. He wasn't sure anyone except children really believed it.

Desma grunted, like she'd heard the folk saying one too many times in her life. Wordlessly, she steered her Kostish closer to the dark opening in the side of the mountain, ready to enter.

Lev raised his blade as a makeshift torch and jerked his head to the cave opening. 'Lead the way.'

The horses slowed to a trot as they entered the caves, the emerald green light casting an ethereal glow over the stalagmites. Lev kept silent, listening for sounds of tunnelling or men's voices as Desma led him through a series of tunnels and caves — but there was no noise at all, other than the echoes of the horses' hooves.

Desma pulled the reigns on her Kostish; the mare whinnied and drew to a halt beside a rock wall so thickly covered in green ivy that the ivy itself had formed a solid barrier, the rock behind it not even visible.

Desma peered into the darkness.

'I don't hear anything,' Lev said. But he knew better than to question Desma's honesty.

'It was here,' she said slowly, pressing a hand to the ivy-covered wall. 'You could hear them … feel the vibrations …'

'Were you heard before?'

'Perhaps.'

'We didn't make a quiet approach just now, either.'

'No. Maybe we spooked them.'

'And you're completely sure it wasn't an Arkod?'

'Don't ask me that again. I know what an Arkod sounds like and I know what I heard: two different things.'

Lev dismounted, giving Huck a firm slap on the flank. He strode over to the ivy-covered wall, blade aloft, the orb of light still illuminating his path. He held out his other hand and ran his calloused fingers over the ivy. He closed his eyes, feeling the ivy's leaves rustle against his fingers, breathing in the crisp scent. His body stiffened.

'What is it?' Desma asked.

'This ivy is distressed,' Lev said. 'You were right.'

His heart immediately began to pump faster. He would have preferred it to have been an Arkod – slaying those slimy-skinned beasts was not Lev's idea of sport, but he'd had more practice at it. Foreign men arriving unannounced in the mountains was not something he'd dealt with since the war.

Lev traced his fingers along the ivy, first to the right a few metres, then back to where he began, then a few metres to the left. Desma's Kostish sniffed his shoulder and he let it, the mare slobbering on the cuff of his cloak while he focused completely on feeling the ivy between his fingers.

Then he raised his left hand and made a controlled, sweeping action with his hand in front of the ivy wall.

At once, the ivy rustled of its own accord, untwisting itself from the rock wall and creeping to the left and the right like a sea parting down its middle.

As the greenery moved away, Lev and Desma were left staring at a wide expanse of grey rock, a large crack running from the ground to the high, icicle-covered ceiling of the cavern.

'Aha,' Lev said triumphantly. 'Desma – are you carrying a weapon?'

'Only my dagger.'

'Ready it, in case. And stay back.'

Desma pulled her mare back, withdrawing a short dagger from beneath her cloak. She held it tightly by her waist. Her face was drawn, but determined, in the emerald light from the sword.

Lev raised his blade and pressed the glowing tip to the centre of the crack in the rock. He breathed slowly, deliberately, absorbing energy from the ivy around him, then bellowed, 'Show yourself!'

The green light from the tip of Lev's sword exploded across the surface of the rock wall, forming a wide arch of green light; then, with a loud pop, the rock disintegrated, collapsing like rain and hissing to the ground of the cave as a deluge of sand.

At once, a chorus of coughs echoed from the other side of the wall.

Lev raised his sword, the glowing tip illuminating a cramped tunnel on the other side. At least three bodies became visible as the dust cleared; some of them held shovels, all illuminated by a couple of dim oil lamps.

'I am Levin Ruck, Deputy Chief of Dervine. Identify yourselves at once.'

One of the men cleared his throat, but didn't step forward from the gloom, remaining as a shadow; he was bearded and heavy-set.

'God's bones, comrade, we're on your side. No need for these shenanigans.'

The voice was gravelly and laconic – like they ought to be sharing a stein of mead.

'I said identify yourselves.'

'Fine, fine.'

The heavy-set man brushed the debris off his black tunic and stepped into the cavern. He had a ruddy face – a drinker – and the thickest eyebrows Lev had ever seen. There were two red stripes on the shoulder of his tunic – they indicated military rank, but it wasn't the same system Dervine used.

'Captain Pavel Pollock of the Paik Ford Regiment of the Peterin Land Army, and these are my men,' he said, extending a hand and peering into the cavern. He glanced at Desma, and Lev's eyes followed – but she had already concealed her dagger beneath her cloak, though her hand didn't leave her side. 'Where's Chief Magnus, then, and why the change of plans? I thought he wanted to meet us tomorrow night.'

Ice hardened in Lev's veins. This was what Magnus knew. But it didn't make any sense. Paik Ford was the closest village to Dervine as the crow flew, but the mountains usually made links between the two shires impossible: they may as well have been separated by an ocean.

The ivy rustled, though there was no breeze here. Lev's brain darted for the right answer, and he decided to play along.

'The Chief sent me in his stead and asked me to receive you first,' Lev said quickly, trying to think up something intelligent to say. He found nothing.

Armed men from Peterin, here in Dervine? Something was amiss. He glanced at the darkened tunnel behind the Captain.

'I see you made it through the mountain, then,' he stumbled, trying not to sound amazed at this breakthrough.

Captain Pollock folded his arms across his chest, inspecting Lev and Desma.

'We did,' he said very slowly. 'Thanks to you blasting out that last bit of rock. Lower that dawn sword, son.'

Lev obeyed at once; he still couldn't process the situation. The emerald orb of light still glowed from the tip of his sword, but now that it was lowered, the cavern was duller.

'Does this mean we get to eat?' one of Pollock's men called from the tunnel.

'I want boiled Kabesh,' called another, raising his voice to address Lev. 'Do you have that in Dervine? I hope it's as good as at home.'

'Our tavern makes a fine roast Kabesh, nice and crispy,' Desma said, defensive at the very assertion that Dervine's meat could be inferior to Peterin's.

'First things first,' Pollock said, rummaging in the inside of his black tunic. He produced a flattened scroll of parchment, the wax seal still intact. 'Here you go, Deputy Chief. Straight from the quill of King Isidor.'

As the scroll was pressed into Lev's hand, the hair rose on the back of his neck. He knew the name Isidor well:

Isidor of Peterin, the rebel son of King Rowan. The scribes had taught him of the tale: how Rowan had exiled his own son during the war for attempting to instigate a coup d'état in the province of Ellence; how Isidor had broken free from his prison in Straida, and now roamed the seas with a band of rogues – a renowned marauder and killer.

The story flashed through Lev's mind in a fraction of a second. So the exiled rebel Isidor was now King of Peterin … there was only one way that could have happened, and it certainly hadn't involved a pleasant chat with his father over some boiled Kabesh.

The rebel Isidor has killed King Rowan, Lev thought. *He has taken Peterin.*

And now he wants to take Dervine, and the rest of Flaran.

Lev's fingers fumbled with the wax seal on the scroll, yanking it open. Shivers of adrenaline were racing down his spine, but he kept up a cool face as Pollock watched him, hands akimbo.

Ink formed narrow, close-together letters on the parchment:

Magnus

I send ahead of me one Captain Pavel Pollock to parlay. All arrangements have been made for you in Takara. You will have two hundred hectares, most of it arable land and well suited to either grazing or agriculture as you wish. A thousand head of Kabesh are yours. Upon completion of our arrangement, five thousand gold denarr will also be yours.

I require your wax seal on this parchment by way of handshake. Once sighted, Pollock's men will arrange your transport to Takara. My troops will then use the new tunnel to occupy Dervine.

TOTK of Peterin, King Isidor II

Lev's heart drummed in his throat.

'I don't suppose you have some kind of portable seal, do you?' Pollock said drily. 'Why'd Magnus send you if you can't sign off?'

Pollock thinks I'm in on it, Lev thought.

The white mare neighed softly as Desma pulled back on her reigns; Desma must have read Lev's body language.

'Magnus sent me to receive you,' Lev said, forcing a casual grin. 'The tavern in town has a crackling fire, much warmer than here, and plenty of salted Kabesh to feed your men. How many are we feeding tonight, just the four of you?'

'Got 'em on rotation, don't I?' Pollock said. 'The others are camped further down the tunnel; these three are my night shift.'

So there's only four of them.

Pollock's eyes met with Lev's just as the flash of triumph went across Lev's face. The smirk on the Captain's bearded face evaporated in an instant, and he reached for his sword.

'No!' Lev shouted in horror as he realised what was about to happen.

Adrenaline pulsed through his entire body in a way it hadn't since the war. The instincts were a little rusty, but they came back. Lev unbuttoned his cloak, letting it drop to the ground and freeing up his arms as he leapt to the right, trying to dodge Pollock's blade as it sliced through the air; the tip sliced his gauntlet.

'TRAITOR!' Pollock roared. 'Men, take them!'

The three men gave a series of battle cries and launched into the cavern: one came for Lev, another for Desma, and a third for Huck, scimitar in hand.

Lev spun his own blade around in haste, the orb of emerald light flinging across the cavern; the globule of light connected with the eyes of the man with the scimitar just as he reached the stallion's side; he screamed as it sizzled his eyes, blinding him instantly.

The orb of light fizzled out, plunging them into semi-darkness broken only by the dim light of the Peterinese men's oil lamps.

Lev whirled his blade around before his body just as Pollock attempted another jab. Lev blocked it deftly: Pollock was muscular, but heavy-set and slow. Lev spun on his heel and slashed at the Captain, who didn't lean away fast enough: Pollock screamed as the steel sliced his back.

The smell of blood reached Lev's nostrils as Pollock stumbled aside, clutching at the cavern wall, while a third man barrelled straight for him, shovel held ready to strike.

Lev held his ground, then pounced to the right at the last possible second; he whirled his blade around and smacked it into the shovel's handle, sending the man stumbling back. He yanked the sword back, but it was embedded in the wood of the shovel's handle; both men were neutered.

'For Isidor!' the man roared, ditching the shovel to the ground and charging at Lev with his bare hands.

Blade still embedded in the wood, Lev abandoned it and brandished his hands together in a smooth motion. A very thin lariat of green light exploded from his palms; he only had time to form a short stick, shorter than a dagger, but it was enough for what he needed.

As the man raced at him, Lev raised the stick and jabbed it straight into his throat.

The man stopped cold, his hands grasping for purchase at Lev's cuirass as his throat gurgled and blood filled his airways. He found an unarmoured stretch of arm and sank in his nails as a final attack, but even the sting of blood couldn't distract Lev.

He yanked the stick out of the man's throat; the man sucked for air for a moment, but only a horrible bubbling sound came as he aspirated on his own blood.

He collapsed to the earth.

'Poe!' a man's voice screamed across the cavern.

Lev stepped back from the man at his feet: the fourth man, who had Desma backed into a corner as her mare whinnied in panic, wore a mask of horror as he watched his friend die. Desma took the distraction as an opportunity, whipping the dagger from her side and planting it deftly in the side of his neck.

She screamed in horror, releasing the dagger as the man collapsed like his comrade, his entire body shaking and fitting.

Lev hunted for Pollock and found him still slumped against the cavern wall, face in shadow from the oil lamp, blood on his hands as he gingerly touched the wound on his back.

'This is treason, Pollock!' Lev roared. 'Isidor is a murderer and a usurper! How could you back him?'

Pollock began to answer, but before he could say a word, there was a scream from behind Lev; the man he had blinded earlier leapt onto his back.

At once, Lev was dragged to the ground by the man's sheer weight, slamming against a sharp rock. His back cracked painfully, winding him; silver stars burst into his field of vision. Blood burned from a gash on his arm.

'Isidor is The One True King of Peterin!' the blinded man declared, wrapping his arms around Lev's neck and tightening his grip. 'He will conquer all the lands in the Halo – starting – with – yours.'

Lev flailed his limbs, but it was useless; the blinded man was wrapping his legs around his own, entwining them and immobilising him with his weight. He struggled for breath, but it didn't come; the muscled arms were crushing his windpipe, pain shooting through his neck.

Frantic, he reached out his right hand, hoping to close it over the sword's hilt – but it was too far away. His hand touched only a strand of ivy.

The ivy.

'Now!' Lev panted, clutching a fistful of ivy and

focusing all his magical energy on it.

At once, the creeping ivy mobilised, rustling along the ground of the cavern towards Lev, slithering en masse in one direction. Lev strained, his vision blackening as the man continued to strangle him – and then he heard it.

'Augh!' the blind man screamed, ivy leaves rustling as the vines wound over his neck once, twice, three times – and then, with a jerk of Lev's hand, they tightened.

The man's grip over Lev relaxed at once; a second later, a spray of warm blood splattered against Lev's back. The man went limp.

Lev sat up, panting, his back aching from the fall – but as soon as the stars cleared from his vision, he saw Pollock standing over him, sword held aloft.

'It's over, Deputy Chief. I just need to know one thing …'

Pollock groaned suddenly, wincing with pain from his back. He steadied himself.

'Either you knew about the arrangement, and Magnus sent you here to double cross us,' he said, 'or Magnus had kept you in the dark, and this was all just a terrible mistake for you. Which is it, before I return you to the earth?'

Lev gasped for air, unable to even formulate an answer. His sword was out of reach, still embedding in the shovel's handle. He was beaten.

'Answer me,' Pollock snarled.

Lev opened his mouth, hunting for some answer to buy time – when suddenly, Desma's shriek rent the air, the brown sleeves of her tunic appearing around Pollock's shoulders, her dagger reaching for his throat, but colliding with his blade.

Pollock turned just in time to avoid the death blow, parrying Desma and sending her reeling back. Lev seized the moment, diving sideways for his sword and wrestling the blade from the wood.

When the blade wouldn't budge, he placed his palm on the wooden handle and used the last wisp of his magic to send a bead of energy into the wood; it relaxed from brown, varnished wood to a soft green stem. Lev pulled the blade from the shovel and scrambled to his feet, sword held before him.

As he rose, he saw Pollock throw Desma to the ground. The Captain turned to finish him, but before he could raise his sword, Desma screamed and reached out, stabbing her dagger cleanly into Pollock's left calf.

The man roared with agony – and in that moment of opportunity, Lev raised his sword and plunged it into Pollock's heart.

Pollock's screams turned to a momentary gasp – and then he crumpled.

A horrible silence reigned. The sickly smell of blood filled the dank air of the cavern. Desma coughed as she pushed herself up. Her gaze scanned the four dead bodies in the cavern. At once, she doubled over, retching violently.

'Come on, we have to go,' Lev croaked thickly, holding a hand to help Desma up. His breath was ragged, his throat still aching. He stared in surprise at the large slash on his arm dripping with crimson; he couldn't even remember who or what had inflicted it on him.

Desma took his hand; her tunic was torn, a graze across the side of her face, but she looked panicked at the thought of leaving.

'The tunnel,' she said, gaping at the dark cavern through which the oil lamps shone dully. 'We can't leave it open – you heard Pollock! There are more of them further back – Peterin's army.'

Lev waved a hand over the cluster of ivy on the ground; it rustled, but refused to move across and block the tunnel entrance like he wanted.

'I can't,' he muttered. He tasted something foul and warm in his mouth; his nose was bleeding. 'Too weak.'

'But – they'll –'

'We'll get men from the village. We need to leave here

now, I'm telling you! I need to see Magnus.'

Lev dragged Desma by the hand further into the cavern; the horses had spooked, even old Huck with his wartime training. They tracked them a couple of turns away and mounted, then Lev led the way back out of the cavern, into the clearing, past the Rock of Rekkor and back down the mountain to the Chief's Cabin.

'Woah!' Lev shouted, yanking Huck's reigns as they reached the cabin at the edge of the village.

Without seeing how far behind Desma was, he leapt off the saddle and raced into the cabin, boots thudding up the spiral staircase as his lungs struggled to catch air.

He charged along the upstairs corridor, drawing his sword. There would be no more knocking at the gnarled wooden door of Magnus' Den: Lev raised his sword and ploughed through the thin door, pieces of wood splintering away as he hacked violently.

Magnus shouted in alarm – the noise had woken him.

Lev reached a bloodied hand through the gaps in the door and yanked the metal bolt open. He threw what remained of the door back on its hinges and strode right up to Magnus' bedside, keeping his blade behind him.

'*Jecarro*, what the shit –' Magnus mumbled, sitting up slowly. The young woman in his bed opened her eyes and shrank against the wall.

Lev hurled the scroll at Magnus, blood dripping to the floor from the gash on his forearm.

'Explain this,' he yelled. 'Explain it, Magnus!'

The Chief didn't even need to open the scroll. The red wax seal bore the insignia of Isidor. He looked up guiltily.

'I told you not to go to the mountain,' he said darkly. 'You should have listened.'

'You sold us out!' Lev cried. 'You sold us – your people – to the pirate Isidor – for your own selfish gain!'

'You can come with me, Lev,' Magnus said. It was the first time he'd used his real name in a long time. 'Isidor is a man of commerce. You can do a deal with him, too.'

'Why?' Lev demanded, staring at Magnus' bulbous nose, stubbornly upturned. 'Why would you do this to us?'

'A soldier like you wouldn't understand!' Magnus bellowed, sitting up higher against the bedhead. His crusty eyes met Lev's and there was a sudden evenness to them. 'Isidor is not like King Rowan. He has rejected the regalia of the Halo. He doesn't abide by our codes of honour.' He swallowed audibly. He was afraid. 'Isidor doesn't negotiate terms with his enemies, *jecarro*. He kills them.'

'So you decided to surrender before he killed you,' Lev snarled. 'He bought you out. You chose gold and sanctuary in a far off land before protecting your own people.'

'I decided not to be his enemy,' Magnus said. 'It was the only way to avoid death. I make no apologies for it.'

'And what about the thousands of people who will suffer under Isidor's rule, if he invades?' Lev demanded, voice breaking with rage. His mind was clouding with incandescent fury, like it did on the battlefield. Words were no longer enough. 'What happens to all of us, while you sun yourself in Takara?'

An uncomfortable smile pricked the edges of Magnus' lips – like he was secretly proud of his manoeuvre. 'I don't know,' he said. 'But it's not my problem anymore.'

'You treacherous *fuck*.'

Magnus swelled his chest in derision. 'You don't talk to me like that, *jecarro*. I am your Chief.'

Fire burned through Lev's veins.

'No,' he said. 'You *were* my Chief.'

Lev raised his sword. The old man didn't even have time to lift his hands in alarm; he sat perfectly still, arms by his side, as the sword swished through the air towards his chest. The girl screamed and dived onto the floor, curling up in the corner of the room.

But the resistance of Magnus' chest never struck the blade. Lev lurched forward, the sword in his hands suddenly lighter than air and soft as petals.

Magnus grinned savagely, yellowed teeth bared, and said, 'Oh, *jecarro*, you shouldn't have.'

Lev blinked and stared at where the sword had been in his hand just a second before. He now brandished a large bouquet of slender, ripe red roses, bound together by a circle of twigs. The crimson petals brushed the corner of Magnus' robe, the verdant stems bent against his chest.

Red-hot terror surged through Lev's veins. In his race to confront the Chief, he had forgotten one crucial element: Magnus was a Peril Mage. His powers, usually uninspiring, were most powerfully unleashed when he was in mortal danger.

Like when Lev had raised the sword to his chest.

Magnus plucked a petal from the bouquet and held it to his nose. 'A sweet scent,' he said, deathly quiet. 'Ah, *jecarro*, look! You made the mistake of an amateur.' He traced a finger along one of the rose stems, now trembling in Lev's hand. 'You didn't remove the thorns.'

Magnus brandished his hand swiftly over the stems of the roses; at once, every thorn was stripped from them and rose into the air, enveloped by a miasma of green light.

Lev dropped the bouquet and lurched backwards as he realised what was happening, throwing his hands over his eyes as Magnus cried out and launched the volley of thorns at his face.

Lev screamed as the thorns speared into his skin, burrowing into his face like leeches and scratching into his flesh. He dove blindly for the floorboards, his thick fingers scrabbling at his face and trying to pull the thorns out – but more flew through the air, slicing his hand.

Lev doubled over onto the wooden floorboards, blood trickling down his face, and then began moving his palms in a rhythmic, circular motion against the floor. The wood glowed with an emerald light; Lev directed it across the room, until all the floorboards beneath Magnus' bed were radiant with the glow.

'NOW!' Lev screamed, directing all his will into the

floor.

At once, the solid, splintery wooden floorboards became young again – limp and green, like a nascent bud. Unable to support the weight of Magnus and his bed, the spongy, living green floor sagged momentarily, and then tore itself apart.

Magnus screamed as the floor disappeared beneath him; his bedframe rocketed through the hole to the ground floor and crashed down onto the stone floor below.

Panting, Lev told the remaining floorboards to harden again, and they did, cracking and crunching as they became dried wood again.

Blood still trickling down his face from the now-stationary thorns, Lev crawled to the edge of the gaping hole and peered down. The bed was nearly destroyed, its limbs mutilated, the mattress rent to smithereens; rogue feathers floated in the air.

Magnus was sprawled, spread-eagled, on the stone floor. A clump of white feathers beneath him looked to have partially broken his fall. A few feathers were speckled with red.

Lev tensed on the edge of the hole, gaze trained on Magnus' body for a sign of movement.

He jumped as the floorboards creaked; he jerked his head around to see the Chief's girl fleeing the bedroom, her sobs muffled against her tunic.

'Lev! Are you alright?'

The panicked voice came from the ground floor. Lev peered back over the lip of the hole in the floorboards.

Desma stood awkwardly at the foot of the shattered bed, eyes flicking between the hole in the ceiling and Magnus' body on the ground. Her dagger was in her hand, though she held it limply.

'I'm fine,' Lev called. 'Desma, stay away from the Chief. I don't know if he's –'

He was interrupted by Desma's shriek.

Magnus' eyes had flown open, his left arm raised in a

circular, conjuring motion. Sparks of green light swirled into lariats, forming a long loop of thick, juicy vine, which the Chief launched through the air at Desma, like a venomous snake unfurling itself for a deadly strike.

The vine wrapped around Desma's neck, crushing her windpipe, before it lifted her horizontally into the air and slammed her body against the stone mantle of the fireplace.

A sickening crack reverberated through the room as her head struck the mantle.

Her limp body dropped to the stone floor.

'Desma!' Lev screamed.

Before he knew what he was doing, Lev hurled himself through the hole in the floorboards, aiming for the largest pile of bed feathers he could see.

His legs crunched as he landed on the feathers and rolled toward the armoury cabinet. Pain sparked up his calves like a thousand pinpricks, but he clambered back to his feet, steadying himself against the oak cabinet.

'STOP, MAGNUS!' Lev roared.

The Chief was miraculously on his feet, his torn robe dangling behind him as he lurched clumsily for the door to the stables.

Rage taking hold, Lev twisted his right hand in a circular motion, forming a cluster of sharp sticks which he launched at Magnus like a rain of spears. Magnus glanced over his shoulder and launched another vine, which whipped two of the miniature spears away; two others ricocheted off the stone floor; and two of them pierced the flesh on his back.

Magnus howled, but still clutched the handle of the stable door — but then another vine snaked across the room, wrapping around his wrist and squeezing his forearm.

Lev whirled around in surprise.

Desma stood in front of the fireplace, flames burning behind her as her body rose into the air, suspended in an aura of golden light. Her skin had the look of used candlewax; her green irises were alight with radiance. Her flaming auburn hair blew back off her face as if energy was radiating from her body. The vine Magnus had used to choke her was still knotted around her neck – but it was now under her control, the other end wrapped around Magnus' arm.

As Lev watched in disbelief, Desma's jaw opened wide, her eyes rolling back in her head as if she were possessed by a demon. With a jagged jilt of her head, she let out a piercing shriek, like the tortured scream of a dying Pekron, and a burst of yellow light rippled down the vine connecting her to Magnus.

The Chief had turned, his face just as slack with shock as Lev's, his eyes tracking the bead of yellow light as it reached the vine tied around his wrist.

Suddenly, the vine began to split apart, multiple green shoots exploding from a single point. A dozen vines, maybe more, sprang forth, wrapping themselves around Magnus. His arms were pulled back from the door; his chest was bound; his neck restrained ... and then the vines wound around his ankles and lifted the plump man into the air.

And in one smooth motion, the web of vines hurled Magnus into the wall, slamming his full weight against the stone before lifting him again and throwing him to the floor.

Desma roared with revenge before the golden glow around her body dissolved in an instant. Her pendulous body dropped to the floor like a stone into a dry well.

For a moment, there was ringing silence throughout the Chief's Cabin.

Then the vines around Magnus' body began to crack and harden, each of them splintering into dust as the Peril Mage shook them off.

Lev gaped, incredulous at the Chief's resilience, yet also incensed that Desma's blow hadn't finished him. He reached into the armoury cabinet, withdrew one of Eddren's old swords and marched across the stone floor to where Magnus was pulling himself up against the doorknob.

'It's over, Magnus!' Lev shouted. 'Stay down!'

Magnus couldn't haul his weight up to his feet. He turned the doorknob, then fell back to the floor, his fat face funnelled into a triumphant smirk.

'As you wish, *jecarro*.'

He threw the door open. At once, a gust of icy wind blew into the cabin, but it brought more than cold: a tornado of alpine leaves swirled through the doorway, as tall as Lev himself.

The leaf vortex swirled and roared, forming a barrier between Lev and the Chief.

'No you don't!' Lev bellowed, grasping Eddren's sword and charging headlong into the vortex.

At once, the razor-sharp leaves began to scour his skin, slicing through with ease. He couldn't open his eyes against the maelstrom. Even his cuirass was barely a protection: these leaves were jagged, serrated, whirling and piercing his skin in a thousand tiny cuts.

'Argh!' Lev crumpled to the ground, curling into himself against the leaf tornado. His breath was sharp and ragged in his throat. He could hear his heart pounding in his ears. The cuts weren't stopping. He could smell his own blood all around him.

I can't beat this vortex with resilience or strength, he thought in a panic.

He thought of the ivy in the mountain cave and knew what he had to do. He screwed his eyes shut tightly and focused his energies on the leaves as they made contact with his skin, felt into them.

You are distressed, he soothed them. *There is no cause for alarm. You belong on the ground.*

The leaves began to whirl more slowly.

To the ground, Lev commanded. His nose opened and

began to gush with blood.

'TO THE GROUND!' he screamed.

At once, the tornado blew out and a shower of crusty leaves rained down onto Lev's back and to the floor. Lev opened his eyes and spotted something shiny among the leaves on the floor – Desma's dagger.

Lev rose immediately, silver stars sparking into his line of vision. His tunic was soaked in blood. His head was spinning, but his legs kept moving – through the door, into the frigid night air between the cabin and the stables.

Magnus was ten feet ahead, his cold, thick fingers fumbling with the stable door. The roar of the blustery wind covered the sound of Lev's boots on the snow: the soldier raced across the yard and reached Magnus while the Chief's back was turned.

He switched Eddren's sword into his left hand and pressed it into Magnus' fleshy neck.

'You should never have betrayed Flaran, Magnus,' he said thickly.

The Chief clutched his thin robe to his body against the cold.

'You should have stayed down, *jecarro*,' Magnus snarled. His face was grazed and covered in pinpricks of blood. 'But, like any soldier, you can't reason what's in your own best interests.'

'I don't care about my own interests,' Lev shot back. 'That's the difference between us.'

He raised Eddren's sword to plunge it into Magnus' neck; but even as he moved to do so, he felt the blade transform under Magnus' spell, becoming a useless fern.

But Lev had anticipated the Peril Mage's *modus operandi*. Without flinching, he raised Desma's dagger in his dominant right hand and drew the blade swiftly across Magnus' throat.

Magnus' body stiffened suddenly, his face twisted in an expression of shock, a crimson line of death forming across his neck.

Undeterred, Lev raised the dagger again and plunged it directly into the Chief's heart.

Magnus crumpled to the snow. By the time his body reacted, limbs jerking wildly as blood blossomed over his silken robe, it was too late. Lev was vaguely aware of the horses inside the stable whinnying in alarm, but he didn't care. He needed to see the traitor die; to know that it was done. Magnus had betrayed them all. He had killed Desma. The only justice was death.

Once the body was still, Lev heard footsteps reach the threshold of the cabin.

'God's arse,' Desma said. 'Is he dead?'

Electricity danced down Lev's spine. He whirled around, sure his ears were playing tricks on him.

Desma stood in the doorway, silhouetted by the firelight.

Adrenaline racing through him, Lev stumbled across the snowy yard to meet her at the door. Her skin had colour in it again; her eyes were green but no longer had the possessed glow of iridescence. She was badly roughed up, her hair tousled and cuts on her skin, but she was clearly alive.

Lev threw his arms around her and pulled her into a bone-crunching embrace. 'I thought you died ...'

Desma coughed. 'I think I did.'

Lev drew back from her. 'The power you had, Desma — it was beyond anything I've ever seen. I think you might be a Peril Mage yourself.'

'Might be,' Desma said. Her eyes were quite wide. 'Although I never knew a Peril Mage could die and come back from it.' She frowned at Lev's quizzical look. 'I mean it. There were a few seconds there where ... I actually can't remember ... but I know I wasn't in this world anymore. *I came back*, Lev. I don't know how. Is there a type of mage that can do that?'

Lev shook his head. 'Never heard of that. I'm sure you were just unconscious.'

He stepped into the cabin; as the firelight illuminated his face, Desma gasped.

'What happened to your face?' she cried, gingerly touching Lev's cheek.

'Thorns,' Lev said, pulling one out painfully. 'A parting gift from Magnus.'

'You killed him?'

'Magnus committed treason. I relieved him of his duties,' Lev said, wiping Desma's dagger on a small unsullied patch of his lower tunic.

He turned to Desma, wincing from the pain – and the raging storm of terror in his mind.

'I am the Chief of Dervine now.'

Desma stared at him for a long moment, her face a mixture of abject horror and resigned acceptance. Then, slowly, she nodded, tears springing to her green eyes.

'Those men … is Dervine at war with Paik Ford now?'

Chief Levin swallowed. 'Worse,' he said. 'Flaran is at war with Peterin.'

Desma's face hardened: a pallid slate of terror. 'Good thing I told you about the noises, then,' she said blankly.

'All of Flaran owes you a debt,' Chief Levin said. 'But now isn't –'

He was interrupted by his own legs giving way. He tumbled to the floor, his fall cushioned by the stray bed feathers, as silver stars exploded in his vision again.

'You're wounded,' Desma cried. 'Badly. You're all cut up! I have potions and bandages in my saddlebags, just wait a moment …'

'I can heal myself,' Lev said sternly, trying to breathe through the stinging of every cut and slice on his body. 'Desma, I need you to ride into town first. Wake Mother Ignacia, and get her to ring the bell in the spire. Make sure *everyone* assembles in the square. I want every man, woman and child there. Once the bell is ringing, get to Stehr's farm and get him to have a Pekron ready for me when I arrive in town.'

Desma nodded. 'Yes, Chief.' She stepped towards the stable door, then reached into the inside of her tunic and withdrew something.

The crown of flowers.

'You kept that?' Lev spluttered thickly. He spat a globule of blood onto the stone.

'Of course I did,' Desma said, kneeling down beside him. 'You gave it to me.'

She broke each of the small lilac flowers from the crown, placing them strategically on the largest cuts on Lev's body, before placing the bare crown of twigs and stems on his head.

'These will help you heal,' she said firmly. 'I'll be right back to fix you up.'

She fled out into the yard for the stables.

Chief Levin slumped on the bloodied bed feathers and shook, his body racked with sobs that didn't reach his eyes. After years dormant, his warrior reflexes had returned without missing a beat. He could kill a man as easily as look at him.

And now was no time to bury those reflexes.

The war was just beginning.

ALSO BY HOLDEN SHEPPARD

The Black Flower (Short Story)

When Nick and Ashlea first meet, they're just two drunk seventeen year olds at a house party. He's a binge-drinking redneck; she's a wild party girl. And every weekend in a country town like Geraldton is an alcoholic's dream.

It's a perfect match – until it isn't.

When tragedy strikes, Ashlea grows up fast. But Nick can't pull himself away from the booze – or the ghosts of his childhood that echo through every part of his life.

With Nick's addiction threatening to destroy their young love, Ashlea delivers an ultimatum – but it has deadly consequences.

THE BLACK FLOWER is a raw, emotional portrait of two teenagers trapped in the chaos of anger, vulnerability and trauma. This story was originally published in the Melbourne-based anthology *Page Seventeen*.

THE BLACK FLOWER is available in paperback. It is also available as an e-book from Kindle, Barnes & Noble, Apple (iBooks), Kobo, Smashwords and more.

ABOUT THE AUTHOR

Holden Sheppard is a Perth-based YA and fantasy author originally from Geraldton, Western Australia. His short fiction has been published in *Indigo Journal* and *page seventeen*. He has also written for the *Huffington Post*, the *ABC*, *DNA Magazine* and *FasterLouder*.

A graduate of Edith Cowan University's Creative Writing program, in 2015 Holden was awarded a prestigious ArtStart grant from the Australia Council for the Arts. The following year, he undertook a mentorship through the Australian Society of Authors, developing his debut novel. He is a committee member of the Peter Cowan Writers' Centre in Joondalup.

In 2017, Holden began releasing his short stories as eBooks: titles including THE BLACK FLOWER, THE SCROLL OF ISIDOR and A MAN are available through Amazon, iBooks, Barnes & Noble, Kobo and Smashwords.

Holden is a discordant confluence of identities: a geeky rocker; a bogan who learned to speak French; and a gym junkie who has played Pokémon competitively. He may be the only writer to switch to decaf and live to tell the tale, and he's quit smoking more times than he cares to admit.

44

CONNECT WITH THE AUTHOR

Want to keep up to date with the latest news and releases from Holden Sheppard?

You can find him on the web and social media at the following coordinates:

Visit Holden's official website:
holdensheppard.com

Like Holden's page on Facebook:
facebook.com/HoldenSheppardAuthor

Follow Holden on Twitter:
twitter.com/V8Sheppard

Check out and follow Holden's blog:
holdensheppard.wordpress.com

Favourite Holden's Smashwords page:
smashwords.com/profile/view/holdensheppard

Follow Holden on Goodreads:
goodreads.com/holdensheppard